The Sick Lion

and
The Hare and the Tortoise

by Val Biro

AWARD PUBLICATIONS LIM

It was a hot day. Lion felt too tired to hunt for his dinner.

It was a hot day. Lion felt too tired to hunt for his dinner. He was getting old and hunting was becoming more and more difficult, especially on a day like this. But he was hungry, so he sat down and began to think.

"How can I look for my dinner without all that running about?" he asked himself.

"How can I look for my dinner without all that running about?" he asked himself. He spent a while deep in thought, and suddenly he had an idea. Lion grinned a very wicked grin.

"I know," he said. "My dinner can come to me!"

"I know," he said. "My dinner can come to me."

He went into his den and when he came out again he was wearing his pyjamas. Soon all the animals in the forest came to see what was wrong with Lion. They were careful not to get too close to him because lions are dangerous animals.

He pretended to be sick and went to bed in his den.

Lion began to limp. Then he began to shiver, and then he mopped his brow. When he was sure that all the animals were watching him, he turned away. He pretended to be sick and went to bed in his den.

The other animals felt sorry for him. "We must go and visit him," they said.

The other animals felt sorry for him. "We must go and visit him," they said. They thought that a sick lion would not be so dangerous. But clever Fox had spied on Lion and seen him grin his wicked grin.

"Take care," warned Fox.
"He might eat you."

"Take care," warned Fox. "He might eat you."
"Perhaps he's right. Maybe we should not visit Lion," said the others. Rabbit, who was the most timid of all, scampered away and some of the others ran after him.

But Cow was very brave. So she went first and knocked at the den door. "Come in, come in!" called Lion from his bed.

But Cow was very brave. "You are such cowards," she said. "Poor Lion is sick and I want to cheer him up." So she went first and knocked at the den door.

"Come in, come in!" called Lion from his bed. He made his voice sound feeble, and the darkness hid his wicked grin.

So Cow went in, but she never came out.

So Cow went in, but she never came out. All the other animals said how brave Cow was, and did not notice that she never came out of the den.

The next day Pig said, "I will copy Cow and show that I am brave," and he followed Cow's footprints into Lion's den.

The next day Pig said, "I will copy Cow and show that I am brave," and he followed Cow's footprints into Lion's den.

The others saw Pig go in through the den door, leaving his own footprints in the sand. The rest of the animals wondered who else would be as brave as Pig.

Goat went in next to copy Pig. But neither Goat nor Pig came out again.

Goat went in next to copy Pig. But neither Goat nor Pig came out again. Only their footprints remained in the sand.

Rabbit and Duck were still afraid to go into Lion's den but Rabbit said, "I am not really a coward. I will copy Goat and go in but I will wait until tomorrow."

Next day Rabbit went into the den to copy Goat, and Duck waddled after to copy Rabbit. Nobody saw them again.

Next day Rabbit went into the den to copy Goat and Duck waddled after to copy Rabbit. Nobody saw them again.

Clever Fox was watching everything from a distance.

Clever Fox was watching everything from a distance. He had seen all the animals go into the den to cheer up the sick lion.

"Lion must be feeling very cheerful by now," he thought, "with all his dinners walking in like that."

Fox stood by the door of the den and called, "How are you, Lion?"

Fox stood by the door and called, "How are you, Lion?" Lion was delighted to hear the voice of another visitor. He licked his lips and grinned his wicked grin, but he made his voice sound very feeble.

"Very poorly," said Lion. "Why don't you come in, my friend?"

"Very poorly," said Lion. "Why don't you come in, my friend?" Lion hoped that Fox would copy all the other animals and come in to be eaten, but Fox was too clever for that. He stood by the door and looked at the footprints in the sand.

Fox said, "Because I am not a copycat! I see all these footprints going in, but none coming OUT!"
So Lion had no dinner that day.

Fox said, "Because I am not a copycat! I see all these footprints going in, but none coming OUT!"

Fox was too clever to follow all the other animals into the den to be eaten by the lion and he went away.

So Lion had no dinner that day.

The Hare and the Tortoise

"I can run much faster than you," said the hare to the tortoise.

Once there was a hare who could run very fast and a tortoise who could only go very slowly, plod, plod, plod.

One day they met in a meadow.

"I can run much faster than you," said the hare to the tortoise.

"Maybe you can," said the tortoise.
"Let's have a race and see."

"Maybe you can," said the tortoise. He was
tired of being teased about being slow, but he
knew one day he would teach the boastful hare
a lesson. "Let's have a race and see," he said.

"How could a plodding tortoise win a race
against me?" said the hare, laughing.

All the animals came to watch the race . . . Ready, steady, go!

All the animals came to watch the race. They put up a starting line and a finishing post and told the hare and the tortoise to stand side by side on the starting line.

The fox called out, "Ready, steady, go!"

The hare ran fast, hop, hop, hop.
The tortoise crawled slowly, plod,
plod, plod.

   The hare ran fast, hop, hop, hop, for he was
the fastest animal in the forest. He ran so fast that
he was soon out of sight.
   The tortoise crawled slowly, plod, plod, plod, for he
was the slowest animal in the forest.

"I have lots of time," said the hare.
He stopped for a rest and lay down to
sleep, snore, snore, snore.

The hare was so far ahead that when he
looked round he could not see the tortoise at all.
"He will never catch up with me," he thought.
It was a hot day and the hare came to a big shady tree.
"I have lots of time," said the hare. He stopped for a rest
and lay down to sleep, snore, snore, snore.

"I must keep going," said the tortoise,
and on he crawled, plod, plod, plod.

Meanwhile the tortoise plodded on steadily. When he
came to the big shady tree he saw the hare fast asleep.

"I must keep going," said the tortoise and on he
crawled, plod, plod, plod. He didn't stop or look round
and soon he saw the finishing post ahead.

The hare woke up, but it was too late. The tortoise had won the race!

At last the hare woke up, but it was too late. He jumped up and ran as fast as he could to the finishing post. When he got there he saw the tortoise crawling past the post with a big smile on his face.

The tortoise had won the race. All the animals were cheering.

"I hope you've learned a lesson," said the tortoise to the hare. "Slow and steady wins the race."